POLAROID

And Other Poems of View

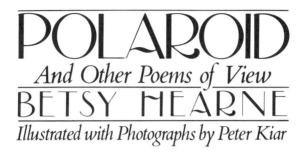

POLAROID
And Other Poems of View
BETSY HEARNE
Illustrated with Photographs by Peter Kiar

Margaret K. McElderry Books
NEW YORK

Collier Macmillan Canada
TORONTO

Maxwell Macmillan International Publishing Group
NEW YORK   OXFORD   SINGAPORE   SYDNEY

1/92- Baker and Taylor - $12.95

Margaret K. McElderry Books
Macmillan Publishing Company
866 Third Avenue
New York, NY 10022

Collier Macmillan Canada, Inc.
1200 Eglinton Avenue East
Suite 200
Don Mills, Ontario M3C 3N1

First edition
Printed in the United States of America
1   2   3   4   5   6   7   8   9   10

Library of Congress Cataloging-in-Publication Data
Hearne, Betsy Gould.
    Polaroid and other poems of view/Betsy Hearne.—1st ed.
        p.   cm.
    Summary: A collection of forty-seven of the author's poems on such topics
as city sights, insights, and relationships.
    ISBN 0-689-50530-2
    1. Young adult poetry, American.   [1. American poetry.]
I. Title.
PS3558.E2554P65   1991
811'.54—dc20   90-45577

To Roger
for his way with wit, words, and kids

Poetry is a way of seeing. We are surrounded by poetic pictures—landscapes, interiors, portraits, still life studies, action shots. Some poems rely on the inner eye, others focus outward. Poetry allows a second look at what may seem, at first glance, too simple to notice or too complex to understand. Any poem with a strong vision sharpens sight. Any keen image—verbal, graphic, or photographic—surprises the eye.

Contents

Outside

City Sights

Close-ups

OUTSIDE

Swans

Through clouds of time they've climbed the sky
and never needed more or less than flying
side by side. The feathered pair and seven cygnets
swim with folded wings through fair
fine silver air of storms spent, fears stilled. Soft
dawn beams of light are slight surprise to
those who float on colors of the sky.

Starfish

Bright with color but blind,
you've tentacled across this tidal
pool all afternoon, seeking new spots
of camouflage after we dislodged
you. With open appetite and no
brain, you trust your feelers to
survive, trust tiny white tendrils
to move your huge orange arms
around seaweed, shells, and stone,
away from unfamiliar human hands.
We have loved you and left you alone,
no small thing for a boy
and a woman too far from stars.
As the tide turned, we tore ourselves
away and walked home.

Starfishes

This one is different, you insisted, too small
to survive the sea, so we took him
    to the kitchen
for a plastic container and created a habitat.
Traveler, we'll name him, and you sacrificed
to the dish of seawater your favorite shell,
which he instantly crawled into and hid.
We cannot keep him, you know, I cajoled,
    he'll die.
You opposed the idea of letting him go,
    checking hourly
his determination to remain immobile,
    with no curl
of an armtip to give you hope. But look, you
called later, he's had babies! In the inmost curve
of shell, almost beyond eyesight, were
    two tiny stars,
reflections of a mother that, subtracted
    from the sea,
added to the universe. You gave them
    water daily,
fresh with the weedy algae we assumed they ate,
and when it was time, released them, all three.

Lakeside Haiku Cycle

Dawn draws a dragon
across the lake mists. Mountains
breathe sun-reddened fire.

The hot sun stops time.
The still lake waits for the first
scarlet leaf to fall.

From water spiders
radiate gray rings of lake,
like lies to oneself.

Trains at certain speed
and distance sound like pine trees
mulling winds' wisdom.

This evening's earth
is blue, spring snow set in a
ring of smokestone sky.

We inch into the
snail shell of midnight, moonpearled,
to the dark's coiled core.

Haiku at Sea

South

Waves swirl away from
the ship sides on white, tapered
toes to dance, rest, rise

North

Wind ships sail by, snow
billowing, but leave frozen
waters unrippled.

Sky Diving

Gulls tear at salmon
clouds swimming against silver
currents of sunset.

Chase

Doe-tailed sunlight flicks
through the glades of afternoon.
A hungry night nears.

Sssh

Spring whispers secret
rain to the listening trees
till they shout loud green.

Dusk

Sun downs, world cools,
but evening still wears day,
a fall-lined coat
of crumbled leaves,
of fog-filled smoke,
of wooly air, of wind
awaiting winter.

Who knows
when night arrives
what guest will bed the earth?
So the blushing sun disappears,
a purple shirt of silk
slipped on his shoulders,
past the tree limbs
lifted in wind blankets
to the will of night.

CITY SIGHTS

HAHA

Polaroid

park
the Siamese cat lady
the Scotch terrier gentleman
    friends from years of enmity
the petticoated infant and bored maid
the thin mother mourning her lost child
the duck family conforming in a liquid line
the kids carving mutinous initials on the bench
the old man wheeled through an airy afternoon
    to ease his extreme stiffness
the forsythia-bordered fountain
sunframed

Suburban Art

Pencil the pearled sky
with broken lines, and fill
them in with flat charcoal
to slow the pathless dash of birds.

Delete the distracting background.
Blacken a square building
over those trees, whose wind-bent
leaves wave shadows on the field.

Graywash the wild weeds
that interrupt cement sidewalks,
toning that stretch of tangled bush
with smoothly synchronized lawns.

Divide the hill in five hundred
elite patches of house,
and over here, the wasted air—
park a breath there.

Do not allow the watching of the world grow
    dark.
Distribute streetlights evenly through your
    night.

Commuters

Like the city skyline they
continue day after day,
bone to dust, stone to sand,
steel to rust, choices
to swaying from straps.

Chicago

As the day is tired,
I, too, will close,
noting with distress
the singular lack
of meadowlarks.

Pigeon Talk

Peacocks scream vain
in the jungle of my heart.
Tangerine parrots chat.

But the even streets
where we must strut
are smooth and hard and gray.

Stones Thrown and Street Cries
(For a Bag Lady)

Song, song, sell me a song
to feed the starving hearts who gnaw
on scraps of a city day,
on the bones of winter unburied—
soot, closed sky, snow.

CLOSE-UPS

Sisters

The oldest, whose time it is to go,
feels thrust out. The child, too young
to leave, is wild to be on her own.
Through the love that laces their hugging
they watch with jealous eyes as one
sets up an apartment to look like home,
the second decorates her room like a disco.

Things

My grandmother's
giving things away,
old things—garnet and gold
rings that fall off my fingers
and roll across the floor,
photos of serious faces
with stories untold, slow
things that her father carved
from wood and bone, lonely
fans, linens folded in fours
and crocheted at the corners
by long-ago friends, tin
boxes locked with tiny keys,
clocks, books, baby cups with silver
dents from children's banging for years.
Her children are quieter now,
tucked into their own houses.
These things of hers are silent.
They fit nowhere in my room.
What shall I do, store them
and close the closet door? They
make the new things look too neat.
Old things are for holding, worn
and torn and mended once more,

softened and smoothed again
in my grandmother's hands.
Now no one has time to hold them.

Geology

Sons of separation,
daughters of divorce,
born between iron and granite,
find it hard to move
without sparks flying,
hard to stay still
without a glacial chill,
hard to chart the hearts
of hostile parents.

Foster Child

You own me till I turn eighteen
and your parental property rights run out.
If I could appeal the court's decision,
I would never give myself away.

You've been mad at me forever.
Whether I was good or bad,
it didn't matter. Now I'm going away,
grown, with my things in a bandanna,
walking slowly from my house of past.

It's calmer since I'm free.
The lumpy couch makes better sleeping
than a haunted bed. My tears are not
for now but then; yet still they hurt to cry.
Look in the mail. My letter spells years
emptied of anger. It costs the grief of seeing
you in me, weighing your worth,
counting your loss. It costs a lot.

Learning Loving

Sometimes I think you think
I'm as rotten as I'm afraid I am.
Occasionally I think you think
I'm as great as I hope I am.
Mostly I trust myself and you
more than I ever thought I could.

Manly Mythology

You've fought or befriended
just about everybody but
you're still warm and wanting more.
Irish in the eyes, New York
in the nerve, tongue on the move,
you jump stairs two at a time—
trouble doesn't come in ones.

If you knew all that's on my mind
you'd load the ark for a long ride,
with marines from your proving ground
lining the rails, room to stow
your Olympian relatives, bunks for
personae picked up on the way,
and a secret garden central in the ship
to meet and love them each.

Whatever mountain you land on
seems yours by laying claim.
You keep it while you live it
and lose it moving on, busy but
for occasions of the heart, of
opening bottles of beer
and shaping hero sagas
from the air.

INSIGHTS

Coco 4 cocoa puffs

Portrait Heartist

You came to me beautiful, begging for photos
to show how you'd model clothes. Yet after
I caught you on camera you cried over coffee,
complaining of faithless friends, your
makeup blurred like an image viewed through
developing solution. Now your glamour
adorns advertisements and magazine covers.
My art fixed your heart in the darkroom.

Listening

My friend has a voice
wild with roses and thorn.
I've hidden in thickets
of her song, surrounded
by their scent, sight, sting.

Practice

Every day is music you have played.
Long light-filled, then sadly swift,
you tune your time and come and go
with grace notes or disharmony,
depending less on notes than sound.

Your count proceeds relentless as
a metronome, you steady moments
on the scale of minor, sometimes
major, modes to shape the song
with measures unknown to your closest kin.

You ache to bend your moments
into song and, singing, lend to men
and women—blend with them—
a note unto itself but soaring, more.
Each day is music you have played. You move
beyond your confines to a greater score.

Trumpeter

The noontime whistle called him back
to work, shook all the melodies from his mind.
He watched men march below his window,
not a shadow scattered on the sill, and, sitting
still till evening, quit his job at the mill.
When he saw the sun go down, he stood
and followed his shadow down alleys
to the godsounds of the band.

Etiquette

Jane Austen, sitting at desk
among family coming and going,
did not reserve her writing
like towered princesses
self-accessible by special
soldiers with saucer-eyed dogs.
Her art was her intimate,
revered as the day come calling,
comfortable with bustle or chore.
And Jane, when visiting art,
never knocked at the door.

Rapture

I don't wish anything much again
but words like those in *The Ginger Man,*
notes like those from Bach's baton,
some paper and pens to write a poem,
your back to lean against my own.

I don't wish anything much again
but to drink, cold mouth on a dripping pump,
to kick away the wooden walls they
started me building with nursery blocks,
to walk in a world as elusive to see
as the wind that's been waiting for me.

Storm

Hold still and hear the rising of the words.
Climb an old stone wall and pause
to feel the rainfall of phrases. Curl
in the shell of a snail poem or sail
on a stanza's kite tail. Strike
with lightning rhymes, and roll
with the rhythms that thunder
when warm beats hit cool minds.

SECOND SIGHT

Sedna

Sedna, an Inuit girl who ran away with a handsome hunter only to discover he was really a bird, became the sea goddess when she was drowned trying to return home in her father's canoe.

Ice floes float farther than Inuit can see,
so Sedna saved us with her body.
Sedna gave us seals and whales while
frozen oceans melted from her tears.
The wails of her father reach us still. She
stretched across treacherous waters with myth.

Penelope

Penelope fended off suitors by saying she would choose one after she finished weaving her father's shroud, which she unraveled each night till her husband, Odysseus, came home from the Trojan War after a twenty-year voyage.

Her name is honor, her word forever,
so she's surprised when he appears
with his beard untrimmed, chest wider,
shoulders heavy with the weight
of the water that carried all his men
to Poseidon, their eyes glazed with salt.
Yes, she guesses she still loves him.
It's hard to remember. Twenty years
is a long time. Not long for honor—she lived
with honor. Honor is a daily event, like
war for some selected Greeks and gods.
Honor showed her what a woman is.
Faith, love, charity can't sustain you when
you're besieged by dishonorable intentions,
by rowdy, drinking, stinking suitors
who haven't a hope of knowing there's no end
to unwinding one's woven shroud. Honor
is an intimate, a sustaining force when fury
fails to straighten the spine after sleepless
nights, the pillow wet with worry for a son

safe only by Spartan standards. Then,
when the tired sun rises, it's honor
that springs the fingers into action at
the day's weaving, at the morning's mocking
      loom.
Honor is the common core, like the dog
that waits beside the door. Now the dog
is dead, Odysseus is here, Telemachus is turning
her away from the heap of bodies arrowed
to the floor. Can honor live with love, can love
survive the tests of self-respect? She looks
at him, at them. Yes, she guesses Odysseus
can stay.

For Whom the Glass Slipper Did Not Fit
(A Cinderella Variant)

From all four corners of the ball swarm
masks, hidden eyes hiding smiles.
The masqueraders whirl, bob, swirl,
reel, squeal, never stay still, dancing
in dresses mimicked from fashion display
dummies.

The clock strikes twelve.
No one leaves. Mummers
pretend to the end, frantic
in patterns that shape them,
plan new garments at a glance,
squeeze into dressmaking molds,
are trimmed.

The clock strikes me.
I see and shrink,
run home alone,
tear away mask and gown,
bathe makeup away in a night
of showering stars,
then sit by the hearth and sigh,
relieved.

Story Born

Beauty and the Beast have discovered their love for each other in tales as old as time, but the voice here is their future child's.

Brute, my mother teases him,
and he rushes us with a roar.
Napping in her lap has left me warm.
Rosie, he calls her, and spills
petals over her head by dozens,
covering me with the scent, hers.
His is sharper, a pungent huntsman
smell still with him after walking wild
in the woods. He takes no one with him
but stalks restless in the wind,
returning softened to our garden, laden
with roses, resting his head on her arm
and holding my short shoulders
against his own. I am flowers and thorn,
born of Beauty and the Beast, and torn,
sometimes, between their sweet and sharp,
between head-sure and heart-fair. Where
is happily ever after, here or there?
The castle is secure, yet leaving it,
alluring. What enchantment keeps me
restless by day but scared of the dark?
Hold my hand and walk me to the park.

Baby-sitting

We were watching "Sesame Street" one day
when everything turned around
    busses backing
    rain rising
    city slowing down.
We rushed to the east to go to the beach
the lake was filled with sand
    fish walking
    people barking
    the water felt dry to my hand.
We went downtown to the city zoo
they locked us up in a cage
    an elephant
    and a wolf walked by—
    I stared back in a rage.
We walked outside to the city park
where pigeons drove cars by.
    The kid I was sitting
    jumped off her swing
    and flew into the sky.

Over the playground,
running to climb,
a shooting star spun round.

But once in a while
    kids' feet forget
    to catch them coming down.
        And then the land
        seems a sad man
        and the sky is surprised by it all.

Rabbit

I don't know how I got stuck
with this job. Easter ducks
I can imagine, chickens, even bugs—
fish understand, being oviparous,
in a way that rabbits never can.
Yet here I am, scurrying around the country
loaded with hard-boiled, fragile-shelled, loudly
colored eggs. Each basket begs to be dropped.

The noses of chocolate rabbits never twitch
with interest. Their ears do not flop,
    softly furred.
I find no kinship with this lot, neither cotton-
stuffed toy surprises nor waxy-grassed beds
of jelly beans. What human has
    mismatched those
who leap and those who plop? Rabbits
    must nest
but not lay. I am way out of my league
    delivering spring.
Four legs, four feet ache, and I understand
    why children
break but don't eat eggs.

Feline Power

The world could use a few more cat habits—
purring when a person's happy,
or putting up the tail when one's in heat
instead of sneaking around about it.
Our leaders could be more honest about
    catching mice,
their movements more graceful, practiced,
with an eye to the playful, a feel for balance.
A subtle touch of noses could save us shaking
    hands.

Spies

My sable cats chase shadows,
sable shadows chase the cats.
They circle on the silent roof
to stalk fall leaves. Both cats and
leaves have scratchy feet and hide
from needling winds that snoop
on spruces. Spruce produces needles
of its own, surrounding nosy street lamps.

DARK AND LIGHT

Escape

If I were sitting lonely in the night
with only my own company to sip
hot cocoa with, as cooking winds
baked early autumn and no lights hid me
from secrets of the dark and blended sounds
of trees and traffic, I would gently dress
my hurt mind not with sleep but shadows,
tuck away lost causes of the day and dance
beneath my hair to rocking rhythms, transform
the world into poems of snowbound peaks,
of Mediterranean ports, of friends I've found.
If you crushed my spicy dreams as cooks
crush thyme in stew, I'd fade to fragrance.

Dreams

During our sleep ghosts walk,
blank-eyed, arms out,
stumbling one on the other,
dropping over hour rims,
reappearing, till light
reseals their eyes and sends
them back, unkempt,
down dimlit corridors of the mind.

Nightmares

Fear creeps in my ear
in spite of lighted, quiet streets,
removing me from reality
to an inner color cinema.

Premonitions persuade me
of anything, alone. Through lamps,
chained doors, and cheerful songs,
shadows stampede my heartbeats.

Did someone leave me long ago?
Only the sight of you disintegrates
gun-firing, knife-slicing, fist-slugging,
thick-tongued, raping fear.

Your locked arms open me.

Observatory

Few feel sun fall over them
as you do at the reach of morning.

So many stay searching through the dark
and starlight of themselves.

Morning at Home

Pot,
how can you perk
so early?
Perceive the stillness
of that spilled
pool of tea,
dotted with breadcrumb
boats.

LONG VIEW

Scheduled

Stop the school.
My songheart is hurting.
Stop the story,
it's ending too soon.
My song is missing the music,
missing walks along the water,
missing my own way
of shaping the days. Stay
home, scrap the lists of musts.
So few warm days of winter!
    I will splinter
    into minutes
    missing,
stopped inside this clock.
The walls are closed,
wheels are turning,
clock strikes twelve,
mouse is running.
Where's it going?
    Outside!
    Can't abide
    time gone time gone time gone time gone time

Statue of a Forsaken Friend

I am toppled in the revolution
of your leaving. Having molded myself
to your making I stood

alone all day all night
as a girl as a slave as an echo
of city sounds around.

My falling shows how
I allowed my hollowing, how
I've been crying rain.

Good-byes

Friends gone, going away,
are the dissolving reality of day,
the heart's experience
of a sinking hourglass.
Pain draws our eyes
to the clock's empty hands
where ticking tells
that the absence of love is death,
that in the rites of life
place marries time.

Empty Sounds

My time yaps,
                clinks,
                        breaks

    like dogs,
            tins,
                    toys.

My heart with you twofold
is halved when you go.

Parlor Shades

The sun stretches light lethargic fingers
across the hours of an aging day,
one of the tapering afternoons
that laces edges to a linen life.

At the last chill flick,
unfolding her hands
from the soft lap of evening,
a lone hour draws closed our afternoons.

Airborne

Flying through gardens of cloud,
reading's impossible, details remote,
duties float away, gray-suited
figures in the seats recede,
fantasies bloom like dew-wet
dormant ferns unfolding from winter.
    Clouds, curls, fronds
    cloud-curled fronds.

Flying over snowmade mountains
reminds the bird of what remains
despite all seasons.
Rivers snake the skeletal desert,
cities blink their feverbright eyes,
and last, a sky-laid sea leaves far behind
flat-patterned farms forever grounded.
    Welcome and good-bye.